anythink

UNDER THE SAME SUN

BY
SHARON ROBINSON

ILLUSTRATED BY
AG FORD

SCHOLASTIC PRESS • NEW YORK

AG Ford would like to thank Sharon and David Robinson for supplying reference photographs of Tanzania, the safari, and the beautiful Robinson family. • Special thanks to Dr. Besi Brillian Muhonja, Assistant Professor of Africana Studies, Women's and Gender Studies, and Foreign Languages, Literatures, and Cultures at James Madison University; and to Erick Amick, Assistant Director of the Swahili Flagship Center at Indiana University, for their insightful consultation of the manuscript and glossary.

Library of Congress Cataloging-in-Publication Data

Robinson, Sharon, 1950–
Under the same sun / by Sharon Robinson. — 1st ed.   p.   cm.
Summary: It is Grandmother Bibi's eighty-fifth birthday, and when she travels to Tanzania from America
to visit her son and grandchildren, they surprise her with a birthday safari. And while visiting an old African slave port,
Jackie Robinson's seven African grandchildren discover how their family came to America.
ISBN 978-0-545-16672-0 (hardcover : alk. paper) 1. African American grandmothers — Juvenile fiction.
2. Birthdays — Juvenile fiction. 3. Safaris — Tanzania — Juvenile fiction.
4. Families — Tanzania — Juvenile fiction. 5. Tanzania — Juvenile fiction.
[1. Grandmothers — Fiction. 2. African Americans — Fiction. 3. Birthdays — Fiction.
4. Safaris — Fiction. 5. Family life — Tanzania — Fiction. 6. Tanzania — Fiction.] I. Title.
PZ7.R567683Afr 2013   813.6 — dc23   2012015732

10 9 8 7 6 5 4 3 2 1   14 15 16 17 18
Printed in China   38
First edition, January 2014

The display type was set in Bad Typ. The text was set in Adobe Garamond Pro.
Maps on page 39 by Jim McMahon.
AG Ford created the artwork for this book using acrylic paintings as his base, then finishing them in oil paint.
Art direction and book design by Marijka Kostiw

For my mom, Rachel Robinson —

an extraordinary mother and grandmother —

on her ninetieth birthday!

And to families everywhere

who are separated by land and sea

With special thanks

to the grandchildren of Rachel and Jackie Robinson:

Rachel, Rahely, Faith, Saburi, Nubia, Busaro,

and Onia Robinson,

for their help in writing this story

— S.R.

Dedicated to

my lovely grandmothers,

Amy Lee Turner

and

Barbara Jean Singleton

— AG.F.

THE SUN ROSE in the sky like an orange ball of fire.

The rooster crowed. Then the dawn light gave way to an early-morning blue.

"Nubia! Busaro! Saburi! Onia! Wake up!" Father called. "Rachel! Rahely! Faith! The plane will soon be landing!"

Today Auntie Sharon and Grandmother Bibi were coming to Tanzania for a visit — all the way from America! Soon it would be Bibi's eighty-fifth birthday! And the children were planning a *big* surprise.

Quicker than lightning, seven children dressed and slipped into shoes and raced out to Father's old jeep. They'd waited all year for this special visit, and they didn't want to be late!

Then off they went to the airport.

Outside the terminal, the family was lost in the crowd that had gathered. But when they saw Auntie Sharon and Grandmother Bibi, they rushed over to greet them.

"Karibuni!" "Welcome home!" "Welcome to Tanzania!" the children all shouted at once.

When they returned home, the house bustled with excitement. Nubia,
Rachel, and Rahely prepared the guest rooms. They made the beds
and hung mosquito netting and curtains.

The children didn't take their eyes off of Auntie's
and Bibi's big suitcases. They knew there were
gifts for everyone tucked inside. But they
would have to wait until after
lunch to see them.

The next few days were spent together exchanging gifts, telling stories, and filling in the gaps from their years spent apart.

The family made frequent trips to the market for fresh mangoes, pineapples, bananas, and greens. Mother made a dinner of *kuku na mchuzi wa karanga*, a delicious chicken dish stewed in a spicy peanut sauce.

Days and nights were hot and steamy. And the children counted

down the time to Bibi's birthday.

Soon they were ready to prepare for Bibi's big surprise.

Clothes were washed. Suitcases were packed.

Two women arrived to braid hair.

"Where are we going?" Bibi asked.

Everyone smiled and exchanged knowing glances.

But no one said a word.

Finally the time had come.

Once again, the family crowded into Father's ancient jeep. Bags were strapped to the roof. But still, everyone kept the secret.

As hours passed, the landscape changed from bustling, dusty city to villages set against lush, green, open countryside. Soon they neared mountain ranges that rose high in the sky, and paved streets gave way to muddy, potholed roads.

As the jeep bounced along, the front wheel sank, without warning, into the mud.

"Everyone out! Put on your shoes! You're walking to the village," Father called out. "You can buy sodas while I get the car out of the mud."

An hour later they were back on the road. And they continued on their long, long journey until Father pulled up to the entrance of Serengeti National Park.

"Surprise! Happy Birthday!" they shouted together.

"We're going on a safari!"

"A safari!" Bibi cried. "This will be the best birthday of my life!"

Tears of joy spilled from her eyes.

The children grinned from ear to ear.

After dinner, the children waited impatiently until the waiters brought out the birthday cake. It was decorated with small wooden animals: an elephant, a giraffe, a buffalo, a hippopotamus, and a lion. A single candle lit their path.

Just as Bibi was about to cut into the cake, a monkey jumped down from a tree and onto the wall next to Saburi. The children fell out of their seats with laughter as the waiters chased the monkey away.

Early the next morning, their guide arrived to pick them up and told them the rules: "The animals may look beautiful and harmless," he said, "but they are still wild! They are not caged like they are at the zoo, but roam freely. On a safari, it is humans who must stay in their cages!

"Lions are known to come into the camp at night. *So no playing after dark!*"

The family piled into the jeep — and their three-day safari adventure began!

The first thing they passed were lazy hippos cooling in ponds.

Exotic birds walked near rough-skinned crocodiles, alert to signs of the crocs coming out of the water.

And soon a large herd of graceful gazelles swept across the plains.

Then the family drove along quietly for a while until Busaro shouted, *"Simba!"*
He pointed to the trees in the distance where a pride of lions rested in the shade. The
lions stretched and rolled over. But they didn't get up.

On the second day, they set out in the barest of morning light. Soon they saw shadows moving.

"Twiga! Twiga!" Nubia whispered. And sure enough, many tall, lanky giraffes loped along the plains. Some stopped to pose for photos as everyone's cameras clicked.

On the third day, elephants lumbered heavily across the road, some sounding their trumpets as they passed. They walked slowly, slowly, their enormous ears flapping with each step. Their trunks scooped hunks of grass into their mouths. Finally, they moved along on their way.

Again the family drove for a time, searching the horizon — when they spotted a herd of zebras thundering in the distance! "Look!" shouted Faith.

"Punda milia!" shouted Saburi at exactly the same time.

On the fourth and last day, they packed up the car and made the long, long trip back home. But before their journey ended, they made one last stop in a small, historic town called Bagamoyo. It stood right beside the Indian Ocean. In it were ruins and a museum that preserved a piece of Tanzania's past.

"Bagamoyo was once home to a slave-trading post," Father told them. "People were captured and brought here with their legs chained together to keep them from running away. 'Bagamoyo' comes from a Swahili phrase that means 'to let go of one's heart.'"

The family listened in silence.

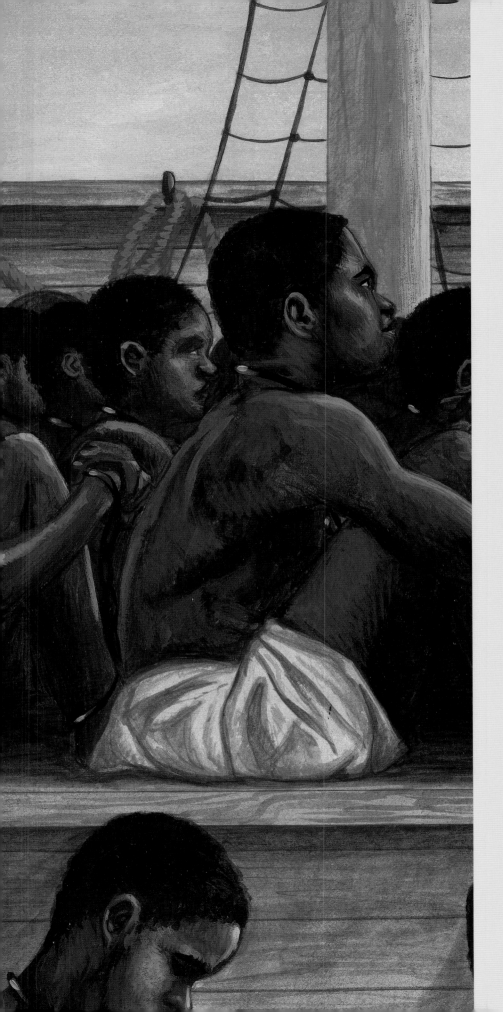

"It was in this place that their hearts were broken," Father continued. "They never saw the African shores again."

"That's such a sad story," Rahely said.

"But, what *are* slaves?" Saburi asked.

"They were the men, women, and children who were stolen from their families and their country. They were shipped far away from their homes and forced to work hard without pay. Many were taken to America," Father replied.

"Was anyone stolen from our family?" Faith asked.

"Your great-great-grandparents were captured on the west coast of Africa and shipped to America, to the state of Georgia. They worked hard in the fields picking cotton until slavery was outlawed."

"But Father, you came back to Africa," Saburi said.

"That's right. I wanted to return to my ancestral past. And, I made our home here with you," Father said.

The family walked silently from the ruins to the water. The Indian Ocean roared in their ears. Laughter and voices of nearby swimmers were drowned out by the ancient spirits of the sea.

As the sun set, they spent their last precious moments together walking along the beach.

"If Bibi goes back to America, I'm going, too!" Nubia announced.

Everyone laughed. But what Nubia had said in her small child's voice was powerful. She had spoken what everyone was feeling. Soon, they, too, would have to separate. It would be a long time until they saw one another again.

"It's fitting that we ended our visit with a trip to Bagamoyo," Bibi said. "I can feel our ancestors' spirits all around us. I can feel their pain in saying good-bye and of leaving their loved ones behind."

"I know what you mean," said Father. "But we are much more fortunate than our African ancestors who were forced to leave the country that they loved and had no chance of returning. We are blessed with the freedom to travel back and forth."

Bibi gathered her children and grandchildren in her arms. "We may be separated by land and sea, but we are always under the same sun," she said. And she hugged them all at once.

"Will you come back for Christmas?" Rachel asked.

Bibi put a finger to her lips, then she and Auntie Sharon exchanged knowing smiles. And together, they began to count the days until they would see one another again.

AUTHOR'S NOTE

Tanzania is far from the Connecticut suburbs where my brother David and I grew up. And it's far from Brooklyn's Ebbets Field, where our father, Jackie Robinson, made history in 1947 by integrating baseball.

But in 1984, David gave up all that was familiar to him — and started a new life in East Africa. He was attracted to Tanzania's magnificent countryside, its rich culture, its stable democratic government, and its connection to our distant past. But there is also much poverty there. Our family commitment to social activism was fostered in us since early childhood. And as the founder of a coffeegrowers' cooperative, David has committed his life to partnering with the people of this region to fight poverty and foster economic development.

Bibi's eighty-fifth birthday. Back row, left to right: Ruti, Onia, David, Faith, Rahely, Bibi, Rachel, Auntie Sharon. Front row, left to right: Nubia, Saburi, Busaro. (2007)

Left to right: Rachel, Faith, Rahely. (2010)

Of the many gifts David has brought to us, his family is surely the greatest. My mother and I can never get enough of them. But making our way there is grueling. We arrive in Dar es Salaam worn thin after forty-eight hours of travel. Instantly, we are revived by seven joyous children and the welcoming arms of David and his wife, Ruti. Nothing matches the thrill of seeing the children, hearing their lilting English and their fluent Swahili — and seeing how much they each have grown and changed.

Nubia (2007)

With our family separated by such a great distance, we find ourselves always aching to be together. Fortunately, our mother, Rachel Robinson, provides the bridge between our African and American families. While I am an occasional visitor, Mom makes frequent trips to Tanzania. For her seventy-fifth birthday, she insisted everyone join her in climbing partway up Mt. Kilimanjaro. On Mom's eighty-fifth birthday, we took her on an amazing safari. That is the trip on which I based this book.

This past year, our loving and strong mom turned ninety. Once again, I accompanied her back to our Tanzanian home. As before, her indomitable spirit bridged the gap of years and distance — and reminded us that we are always together under the same sun.

Left-hand picture, from top to bottom: Saburi, Busaro, Onia. (2007)

Right-hand picture: Bibi's ninetieth birthday visit. Back row: Bibi and David. Front row, left to right: Saburi, Busaro, Onia. (2012)

Same kids, five years later! See how fast they grow!

TRAVELING TO TANZANIA

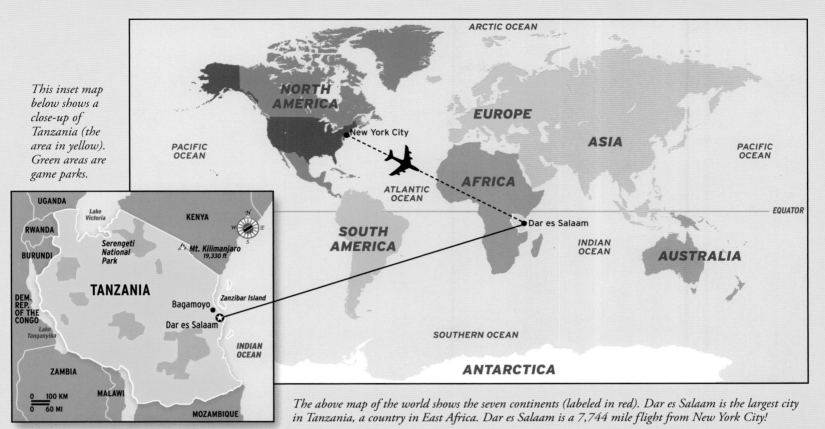

This inset map below shows a close-up of Tanzania (the area in yellow). Green areas are game parks.

The above map of the world shows the seven continents (labeled in red). Dar es Salaam is the largest city in Tanzania, a country in East Africa. Dar es Salaam is a 7,744 mile flight from New York City!

SPEAK SWAHILI

The Swahili language, or Kiswahili, is a Bantu language widely spoken in East Africa.

It is the official language of Tanzania, and the language of my brother's family.

David's jeep on the way to the safari.

Bibi (BEE-bee)	Grandmother
Shangazi (shan-GAH-zee)	Aunt
Baba (BAH-bah)	Father
Mama (MAH-mah)	Mother
Karibu (kah-REE-boo)	Welcome
Karibuni (kah-ree-BOO-nee)	Welcome to several people
Simba (SEEM-bah)	Lion
Twiga (TWEE-gah)	Giraffe
Tembo (TEM-bow)	Elephant
Punda milia (POON-dah mee-LEE-ah)	Zebra
Kuku na mchuzi wa karanga (KOO-koo na M-CHU-zee wa KA-rahng-gah)	Chicken and peanut stew
Bagamoyo (bah-gah-MOH-yoh)	A small coastal town north of Dar es Salaam. The name comes from two Swahili words. Bwaga (BWAH-gah) means "to release; to let fall; to lay down." Moyo means "the heart." Some believe the name refers to the slaves who came through, giving up all hope. Others believe it derives from the porters, of a different time, who rested in the town after carrying heavy cargo.

Pineapples at a roadside stand.

A TANZANIAN MEAL

Cooking with my family is an adventure. Food is bought fresh several times a week from open outdoor markets. It is lovingly prepared, and can take hours as things are pounded with mortar and pestle and cooked outside on a coal stove. Coconut meat is pounded by hand, mixed with water, and strained to make fresh coconut milk. The stringy, tough leaves of the cassava plant are pounded and cooked and mixed with coconut milk, sautéed peppers and onions, and spices. On our last night together we made fish with coconut sauce. It is one of our favorite dinners.

The roadside stand with fresh produce (left), and the open outdoor market (right) where we shopped for our dinner.

The coal stove is ready to grill the fish.

Rachel cuts green peppers for the vegetable dishes.

Busaro, Ruti, Nubia, and Rachel get ready to prepare the rice. (2012)

Grilled fish, coconut sauce, cassava greens, carrots with peppers and onions, rice, and a fresh salad. A delicious ending to a wonderful visit!